Dear Parent:
Your child's love of reading starts here!

Every child learns to read in a different way and at his or her own speed. Some go back and forth between reading levels and read favorite books again and again. Others read through each level in order. You can help your young reader improve and become more confident by encouraging his or her own interests and abilities. From books your child reads with you to the first books he or she reads alone, there are I Can Read Books for every stage of reading:

SHARED READING
Basic language, word repetition, and whimsical illustrations, ideal for sharing with your emergent reader

BEGINNING READING
Short sentences, familiar words, and simple concepts for children eager to read on their own

READING WITH HELP
Engaging stories, longer sentences, and language play for developing readers

READING ALONE
Complex plots, challenging vocabulary, and high-interest topics for the independent reader

ADVANCED READING
Short paragraphs, chapters, and exciting themes for the perfect bridge to chapter books

I Can Read Books have introduced children to the joy of reading since 1957. Featuring award-winning authors and illustrators and a fabulous cast of beloved characters, I Can Read Books set the standard for beginning readers.

A lifetime of discovery begins with the magical words **"I Can Read!"**

Visit www.icanread.com for information
on enriching your child's reading experience.

I Can Read!

PONY SCOUTS

The Trail Ride

Pony Scouts: The Trail Ride
Copyright © 2012 by HarperCollins Publishers
All rights reserved. Printed in the United States of America. No part of this book may be used or reproduced in any manner without written permission exc
in the case of brief quotations embodied in critical articles and reviews. For information address HarperCollins Children's Books, a division of
HarperCollins Publishers, 10 East 53rd Street, New York, NY 10022.
www.icanread.com
Library of Congress catalog card number: 2011927589
ISBN 978-0-06-208671-6 (trade bdg.)—ISBN 978-0-06-208670-9 (pbk.)
Graphic design by Sean Boggs

12 13 14 15 16   LP/WOR   10 9 8 7 6 5 4 3 2   ❖   First Edition

PONY SCOUTS

The Trail Ride

by Catherine Hapka
pictures by Anne Kennedy

HARPER

An Imprint of HarperCollinsPublishers

Jill, Meg, and Annie

are the Pony Scouts.

They were taking a riding lesson

at Jill's family's pony farm.

"Steer your ponies around the cones,"

Jill's mom told them.

"As soon as you can steer
well enough,
you can go on a trail ride."
"That sounds like fun!"
Meg said.

Just then a truck drove in.

"Who's that?" Annie asked.

"It's the farrier," Jill said.

"He trims the ponies' hooves
and puts on their shoes."

"Oh, dear," her mom said.

"I thought he was coming later.
I asked him to put new shoes
on Inky and Smoky today."

"Mom's taking Inky and Smoky
to a horse show tomorrow,"
Jill told her friends proudly.
"Can you girls ride without me
for a little while?" her mom asked.
"I'll just be right in the barn."

"We'll be fine, Mom," Jill said.

"I'll help Meg and Annie practice their steering."

"Okay," her mom said.

"But no trotting until I get back."

"It's weird riding without
your mom here," Annie told Jill.
They rode around the cones again.
"Good job!" Jill said.
"Should we trot now?" Meg asked.
"No!" Annie said. "Jill's mom
said we're not allowed, remember?"

They walked around the cones again.

Meg wished they could do something

a little more exciting

than walk around cones.

"I have an idea!" she said.

"Your mom said

we could go on a trail ride

when we knew how to steer,"

Meg reminded Jill.

"You just said we're doing great.

So let's go on a trail ride now!"

Annie gasped. "By ourselves?"

"Sure," Meg said.

"She'll be proud of us.

Come on. Let's go!"

Meg rode out of the ring.

Jill followed on her pony.

"I guess it will be okay," she said.

"But we'd better stay on the trail

right behind the pastures."

Annie was worried.

But she didn't want to be left behind.

She followed her friends.

The three of them rode

into the woods near the riding ring.

"This is great!" Meg said.

Jill smiled. "I love trail riding.

Mom and I do it all the time."

Annie still felt nervous.

But she was having fun, too.

The girls rode along the trail.

They saw birds and squirrels.

They rode up and down hills

and practiced their steering

on all the curves.

Jill led the way on Apples.

Then Meg's pony turned off the trail.

Meg giggled. "Sparkle thinks

we should go this way!"

The girls rode

into a meadow.

Suddenly a bird flew up

beneath Sparkle's feet.

"Whoa, Sparkle!" Meg cried

as her pony jumped to one side.

Seeing Sparkle spook

made Annie nervous.

"We should go back," she said.

Meg was sad.

She wanted to trail ride all day!

But Jill looked worried.

"Mom might be mad

that we rode so far," she said.

"Let's go back," Annie said.

"Where's the trail home?"

Jill looked around and gulped.

The trees looked the same

in every direction!

"I'm not sure," she said.

"Are we lost?" Annie cried.

"Oh, no!" Meg said.

"How will we ever find our way home?
Your mom might have to call
the police to find us!"

For a second Jill was worried, too.

Then she remembered something.

"Don't worry, you guys," she said.

"The ponies always know how

to find their way home!"

"Are you sure?" Annie asked.

Jill nodded. "Watch," she said.

She loosened her reins

and gave Apples a gentle kick.

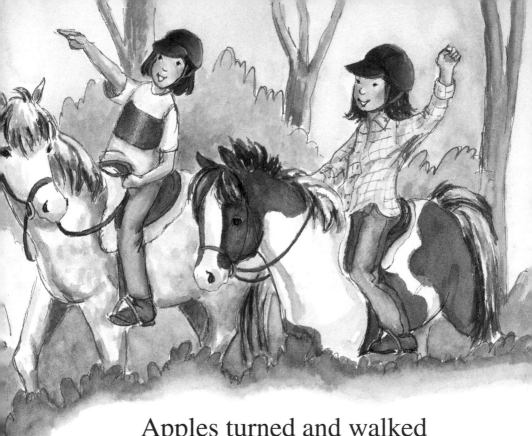

Apples turned and walked

into the woods.

The other ponies followed.

"We passed that tree before!"

Meg exclaimed.

"Hooray for smart ponies!"

Annie cheered.

The ponies went back to the farmyard.

"What happened?" Jill's mom cried.

"We went on a trail ride," Jill said.

"We thought you wouldn't mind."

Meg nodded.

"We didn't trot," Annie added.

Jill's mom wasn't happy.
She reminded them that Meg and
Annie were still new to riding.
Trail riding without an adult
could be dangerous.

"I'm sorry," Meg said.

"It was all my idea."

"No, we all agreed to go," Jill said.

Annie nodded.

"Pony Scouts stick together,"

she said.

"All right," Jill's mom said.

"But from now on,

please check with me first

when Meg has an idea."

"We promise," Jill and Meg said.

"Pony Scout's honor!" Annie added.

PONY POINTERS

farrier: A person who trims a horse's or pony's feet and puts on horseshoes if needed. Sometimes also called a blacksmith or a horseshoer.

trail ride: Riding outside of a riding ring, often on a trail through the woods

spook: What happens when a horse or pony is startled or frightened. He or she might jump in place, spin around, or run away.